David McKee
KING ROLLO'S PLAYROOM
and Other Stories

D1512994

BEAVER BOOKS

Also available in Beaver by David McKee

The Adventures of King Rollo
Further Adventures of King Rollo
Not Now, Bernard
Tusk Tusk
The Hill and the Rock
I Hate My Teddy Bear
King Rollo's Letter and Other Stories
Two Can Toucan
Two Monsters

A Beaver Book
Published by Arrow Books Ltd, 62-5 Chandos Place, London WC2N 4NW
An imprint of Century Hutchinson Ltd
London Melbourne Sydney Auckland Johannesburg
and agencies throughout the world
First published by Andersen Press 1983
Sparrow edition 1984 Beaver edition 1987
© David McKee 1983
All rights reserved. Printed in Italy by Grafiche AZ, Verona
ISBN 09 933080 6

KING ROLLO

and the playroom

"What are you doing?" King Rollo asked Cook.

"I'm tidying your playroom," said Cook.

"Why don't you put things away when you've finished with them?" she asked.

"I might need them again later," said King Rollo.

"Anyway, I like it untidy. Leave this room alone," he said.

"All right," said Cook, and she left.

"Good," said King Rollo and he played with his bat and ball.

Then he played with his toy soldiers.

Then he played with his bow and arrow.

Then he read a book.

Then he tried his boxing gloves.

Then he painted a picture.

Then he played with his train.

By the time he left the room King Rollo had played with lots of things.

That night he slept very well.

The next day King Rollo went back to the playroom.

"Where's the book I was reading?" he said.

He stepped on some soldiers and broke one.

He knocked over his paint pot.

He snapped an arrow.

Then he found the book. It was spoilt by paint.

A little later the magician looked into the room.

"What are you doing?" the magician asked King Rollo.

"Tidying my playroom," said King Rollo.

KING ROLLO

and the breakfast

King Rollo woke up and felt hungry.

"I think I'll have breakfast in bed today," he said and rang for Cook.

The magician came in. "Cook is ill," he said.

"Who will get breakfast?" asked King Rollo.

"I can't worry about breakfast. I'm off to get the doctor," said the magician.

King Rollo got out of bed.

He washed himself.

He dried himself.

He got dressed.

Then he went downstairs to the kitchen.

"First put on the kettle," King Rollo said to himself.

"Bread for the toast," he said and started the toaster.

"Oh dear! Where are the eggs?"

"And I'll need the jam," he said.

Upstairs in bed Cook opened her eyes. "Oh dear," she said as she heard the boiling kettle.

"Oh dear, oh dear!" she said as she smelt the burning toast.

"Oh dear, oh dear, oh dear!" she said as she heard something fall.

Then there was a knock on the door. "Come in," said Cook.

King Rollo peeped around the door. "It's about breakfast," he said.

"Oh, I really can't make it today," said Cook.

"No," said King Rollo, opening the door. "I've made some for you."

"You are kind," said Cook. "It's years since I had breakfast in bed."

"But this is far too much for me," said Cook.

"I know," said King Rollo. "I'm having mine up here with you."

KING ROLLO

and the dog

King Rollo was in the garden when King Frank arrived with his dog.

"What a beautiful dog," said King Rollo. "Let's show him to Cook."

They ran indoors with the dog.

"Yes, yes, very nice," said Cook. Then she saw their muddy footprints.

"Out you go," said Cook.

They went to show the dog to the magician.

"Just what I needed," said the magician.

"Why don't you take the dog for a walk?" asked the magician.

They went outside to take the dog for a walk, only most of the time it was a run.

They saw other people out with their dogs.

King Frank told King Rollo the names of the different kinds of dogs.

King Frank knew lots about dogs.

He made the dog beg to say please.

They threw a ball and the dog brought it back.

They chased the dog.

The dog chased them.

At last they were completely tired out.

"Come back and have tea with us," King Rollo said to King Frank. "Queen Gwen will be there."

"I can't," said King Frank. "Before I have tea I must clean and feed the dog."

"You'll starve," said King Rollo and waved goodbye to King Frank and the dog.

At tea King Rollo was still talking about the dogs he had seen.

"I've learnt a lot about dogs," he said.

"Do you know which is the best kind?" asked Cook.

"Yes," said King Rollo. "Someone else's."

KING ROLLO

and the mask

"What are you doing?" the magician asked King Rollo.

"I'm making a mask," said King Rollo.

"King Rollo is making a mask," the magician said to Cook.

"Making a mess is more like it," said Cook.

"Hello, King Rollo, what are you doing?" asked Queen Gwen.

"I'm making a mask," said King Rollo. "Grrrrr!"

"Oh, that looks fun—let me make one," said Queen Gwen.

"Well at least the masks are keeping them quiet," thought Cook.

"GRRRRR!" went King Rollo and Queen Gwen.
"OH MY! OH MY!" screamed Cook.

King Rollo and Queen Gwen ran off to catch the magician.

"GRRRRR!" they went together.
"Morning," said the magician. "Have you seen King Rollo and Queen Gwen?"

"They went that way," pointed King Rollo.

"Good," said the magician and went the other way.

"Let's make some more masks," said Queen Gwen. "I'll make one like you, you make one like me."

They'd just finished when they heard Cook coming so they put on the masks.

"Hello, King Rollo," said Cook to Queen Gwen. "Hello, Queen Gwen," she said to King Rollo.

"Ha, ha!" they said. "Let's trick the magician—let's make two like Hamlet."

A little later they crept up behind the magician.

"GRRRRR!" said the magician. He had a huge mask on.

"AAAAAH!" shouted King Rollo and Queen Gwen.

Then they all took off their masks and laughed just as Cook arrived.

"Come along," she said. "Take off those horrible masks and get your lunch."

"Masks? But we aren't wearing masks," said King Rollo.

"HA, HA, HA! Just a little joke!" laughed Cook.

Other titles in the Beaver/Sparrow Picture Book series:

An American Tail

The Bad Babies Counting Book Tony Bradman and Debbie van der Beek

Bear Goes to Town Anthony Browne

The Big Sneeze Ruth Brown

Crazy Charlie Ruth Brown

The Grizzly Revenge Ruth Brown

If At First You Do Not See Ruth Brown

Our Cat Flossie Ruth Brown

Harriet and William and the Terrible Creature Valerie Carey and Lynne Cherry

In the Attic Hiawyn Oram and Satoshi Kitamura

Ned and the Joybaloo Hiawyn Oram and Satoshi Kitamura

What's Inside? Satoshi Kitamura

The Adventures of King Rollo David McKee

The Further Adventures of King Rollo David McKee

The Hill and the Rock David McKee

I Hate My Teddy Bear David McKee

King Rollo's Letter and Other Stories David McKee

King Rollo's Playroom David McKee

Not Now Bernard David McKee

Two Can Toucan David McKee

Two Monsters David McKee

Tusk Tusk David McKee

The Truffle Hunter Inga Moore

The Vegetable Thieves Inga Moore

Babylon Jill Paton Walsh and Jennifer Northway

Robbery at Foxwood Cynthia and Brian Paterson

The Foxwood Treasure Cynthia and Brian Paterson

The Foxwood Regatta Cynthia and Brian Paterson

The Foxwood Kidnap Cynthia and Brian Paterson

The Tiger Who Lost His Stripes Anthony Paul and Michael Foreman

The Magic Pasta Pot Tomie de Paola

Mary Had a Little Lamb Tomie de Paola

We Can Say No! David Pithers and Sarah Greene

The Boy Who Cried Wolf Tony Ross

Goldilocks and the Three Bears Tony Ross

The Three Pigs Tony Ross

Terrible Tuesday Hazel Townson and Tony Ross

There's A Crocodile Under My Bed Dieter and Ingrid Schubert

Emergency Mouse Bernard Stone and Ralph Steadman

Inspector Mouse Bernard Stone and Ralph Steadman

Quasimodo Mouse Bernard Stone and Ralph Steadman

The Fox and the Cat Kevin Crossley-Holland and Susan Varley

Crocodile Teeth Marjorie Ann Watts

The Tale of Fearsome Fritz Jeanne Willis and Margaret Chamberlain

The Tale of Mucky Mabel Jeanne Willis and Margaret Chamberlain